Zack Attack

Adapted by M.C. King

Based on the television series, “The Suite Life of Zack & Cody”, created by Danny Kallis & Jim Geoghan

Based on the episode written by Bill Freiberger

New York

 For information address Disney Press, 114 Fifth Avenue, New York, New York 10011-5690.

Printed in the United States of America

First Edition
3 5 7 9 10 8 6 4 2

Library of Congress Catalog Card Number on file.

ISBN 0-7868-4938-X
For more Disney Press fun, visit www.disneybooks.com
Visit DisneyChannel.com

Chapter 1

Every home has its own set of rules. Zack and Cody Martin's home was no exception. Only their home was the Tipton, the most luxurious hotel in Boston.

Zack and Cody knew they weren't supposed to play basketball in the Tipton's lobby, which was grand, to say the least. But there was something so satisfying about dribbling the ball on the hard marble floors.

And when Zack tossed the ball to Cody, the antique chandeliers made a really cool clinking sound.

Zack and Cody lived at the Tipton because their mother, Carey, was the lounge singer there. If Carey wasn't working, she was often rehearsing, leaving the rule-enforcing to the other people who worked in the hotel. The Tipton's manager, Mr. Moseby, was the biggest stickler for rules.

Mr. Moseby had a habit of seeing and hearing everything. And within seconds of Zack and Cody entering the hotel, he appeared before them—just as Cody was throwing the ball to Zack. Despite his constricting fancy uniform, Mr. Moseby was quick: he caught the basketball in midair. He held on to it, shaking his head disagreeably at the two boys. "No b-ball today," he said with a grimace. "Game has been canceled on account of . . . this is a hotel."

Cody shuffled his feet shamefully during the scolding. He and Zack were twins, but he was the younger of the two and also the more rule-abiding. He didn't relish getting in trouble, like Zack did.

The Tipton was not only fancy, it was also one of the largest hotels in Boston. Businesses often rented conference rooms for meetings or held special events in the ballrooms. Usually, the events were *really* boring. Take last week's annual podiatrist convention. Cody had needed to look "podiatrist" up in the dictionary to discover what it meant: a doctor who specialized in feet. (Who'd wanna specialize in feet?)

So Zack and Cody were very surprised when Mr. Moseby cut short his lecture on no basketball in the lobby to say: "Now listen up. *Go Dance USA* is coming to the Tipton for their local broadcast. And it is my greatest wish that you do not scare them away with your antics or . . ." He wriggled his nose in dissatisfaction at Zack and Cody's sweaty after-school clothes. ". . . your odor."

Zack and Cody couldn't believe it. *Go Dance USA* was one of the best shows on television! "We'll do our best not to stink, Mr. Moseby," promised Zack.

"Splendid," Mr. Moseby replied wearily, and walked away.

Zack and Cody's friend Max had come home with them after school. It just so happened that Max was the best dancer at their school, so she was even more excited than the twins to hear Mr. Moseby's announcement. "I can't believe *Go Dance USA* is coming here. I've wanted to go on that show since I was a kid!" Max went to check out the *Go Dance USA* poster that had been put up in honor of the event; the twins followed.

"Max, you have to enter that contest," said Cody. "You're better than that girl in the Missy Elliot video."

"I know, this could be my big break!" Max said dreamily. She took a moment to examine the poster. The rules for participants were listed at the bottom. Oops, they'd missed one detail. "But it's for couples," Max informed the boys. "Zack, would you be my partner?"

Cody couldn't believe his ears! Here he'd been talking Max up, and she was choosing Zack as her partner! Without even considering Cody. "Him?" Cody balked incredulously, motioning to Zack. "What about the guy who just said how good you are?"

"Do you dance?" Max asked Cody.

Did he dance?! "I love to dance," exclaimed Cody.

"Too bad you're no good," teased Zack. "I'll be your partner," he offered Max. "I'd love to be on TV. And I've got the face for it."

Oh, please! thought Cody. "I have the same face!" he argued.

"Yeah, but your face can't dance," said Zack.

Arrrgh! Zack could be so full of himself sometimes! Who did he think he was? Why, Cody oughta . . . An angry Cody took a step toward his brother.

Max took it upon herself to break the brothers up. "Boys, please," she begged. "We'll have a fair and impartial audition. Zack, let's see what you got."

Zack was happy for the chance. "Check it," he told Cody, and launched into a series of music-video-style hip-hop moves.

"Yeah?" said Cody, certain he could top that. "Well, watch this." Cody did a version of the robot—if the robot was a total spaz. He ended up lying face forward on the lobby carpet. Cody might be a fighter, but he knew when to give up. "Good luck in the dance contest, guys," he mumbled.

Chapter 2

For most kids, Maddie Fitzpatrick had the ideal after-school job: she worked at the candy counter in the Tipton lobby. But Maddie knew that nothing made you lose your sweet tooth faster than being surrounded by the stuff day after day. Sure, she'd indulge in the occasional chocolate bar, and she saw it as her duty to taste test the jelly beans when they came out with a new flavor. But mostly, she stayed away from the stuff.

Maddie spent much of her time behind the counter catching up on her homework. In fact, she was such a good student that she usually managed to finish all of it before her shift was up. Sometimes, she even got to the extra-credit assignments.

That is . . . when she wasn't being interrupted by Cody, Zack, or, worst of all . . . London.

London was none other than London Tipton, heir to the Tipton fortune. Her parents owned the hotel, and London lived in its most deluxe suite. She got whatever she wanted when she wanted it. A two-hour hot stone massage? Just call the hotel spa. A foot rub and a pedicure, with a different color on each toenail? Page the hotel salon. A butterscotch sundae at midnight?

Speed-dial room service. Even if the kitchen was closed and out of butterscotch, and the night concierge had to run to the 24-hour grocery store across town to buy it . . .

Maddie and London were both fifteen. While Maddie went to the local public school, London attended a posh private school. Maddie worked hard at everything she did, London worked hard at nothing. They were opposites in almost every way, yet somehow they'd managed to forge a friendship . . . although Maddie wasn't exactly sure that's what she'd call it.

London sauntered over to the candy counter, not bothering to say hello or how are you before launching into her big news. "Guess who's going to be a celebrity fashion judge at *Go Dance USA*?"

Maddie really didn't feel like dealing with

London today. "Guess who doesn't care?" she replied.

London ignored Maddie's sarcastic tone. "It's me!" she yelped. "But I don't have shoes yet. Want to go shopping with me and tell me which pair looks most fabulous on me?"

"As tempting as that sounds, I can't," growled Maddie. "See, I'm working overtime to make money to send my parents to Paris for their twenty-fifth anniversary. It's the honeymoon they never had."

This information didn't seem to move London. "So, you wanna go shopping, or what?" she asked.

Sheesh! Was London for real? "No," answered Maddie. "All my brothers and sisters are chipping in. And if I don't come up with my share before the weekend, the trip's not going to happen."

"Well, how much do you need?"

"Two hundred and fifty dollars," answered Maddie with a sigh. "It's a lot of money."

"It is?" asked a confused London. Her weekly allowance was four times that, so to her that seemed like pocket change.

"Yes, for people who work for a living," Maddie said sharply. She was trying to be patient, but please. . . .

"That's so sad," said London, frowning. "People work all day to make that little?"

"All week!" Maddie shot back.

London was shocked. But clearly there was an easy answer to all of this. "So, if I gave you the money, you'd go shopping with me?" she asked.

"I can't let you give me that kind of money," argued Maddie. She had a tendency to be very proud.

"Why not? I got it right here." London pulled a wad of twenties from her jeans pocket. Or was that a hundred-dollar bill? Maddie wasn't sure—she'd barely ever seen one before.

All that cash! It had an odd effect on Maddie. She could barely speak. "Well, because, I, uhh . . ." she stammered. "I—I don't know when I'd be able to pay you back."

"Don't worry about that. We can work that out. I just need someone to tell me how fabulous I look in my new shoes." London placed the money in Maddie's quivering palm.

Just the touch of all those crisp new bills had Maddie's mind reeling. She imagined her parents, her poor overworked, tired parents, who hadn't taken a vacation in years, boarding a shiny jet plane. Then she imagined them in Paris: her dad sitting at a café, munching on a croissant . . . her mom in a hat shop, trying on a beret . . . the two of them gazing up at the Eiffel Tower, all lit up at night. . . . It was too much. Maddie couldn't resist. London's money would make it all so easy. . . . "I'm your gal!" she gulped a little too eagerly. "Now I just have to get Moseby to let me off."

"I'm *your* gal," countered London, who liked to think she had the hotel staff at her beck and call. She grabbed the CLOSED sign and placed it on the counter. For London, it was that simple.

Well, if that was all it took . . . "Let's go," said Maddie with a shrug. As she walked, she could feel the two hundred fifty dollars in her pocket.

"After me," said London in the most gracious tone she could muster.

Chapter 3

Before Zack and Max could devise a winning dance routine, they needed to pick a song. They'd been going through CDs for the last half hour. Meanwhile, Cody was nursing his bruised ego, not to mention his bruised butt cheeks, with a marathon videogame session.

"Hey, guys." Carey entered the suite, a bag of groceries in her arms.

"Mom!" Zack practically squealed. "I'm gonna be on TV!"

A panicked Carey nearly dropped the groceries on the floor. "What did you set on fire?" she asked, a look of doom in her eyes.

"Nothing," said Zack with a smirk. He wasn't insulted that his mom assumed he was up to no good. "Max and I signed up for a dance contest."

"The *Go Dance USA* one?" asked Carey, breathing a sigh of relief. "Good for you."

"Yeah," said Zack. "We're gonna go downstairs and practice for a couple of minutes."

"Oh, it's going to be a lot more than a couple of minutes," Max interjected. "Dancing is work. Agonizing, grueling work. We're gonna practice until our feet bleed."

With that, Carey grabbed a CD and

whisked Zack out of the suite. She waved good-bye, telling them to have fun.

It was then that she noticed Cody, slumped on the couch, his eyes locked on the television screen. “Hey, buddy, why the long face?”

“Zack’s better at everything than me,” Cody groaned. “Basketball, skateboarding, guitar, and now dancing . . . what am I good at?”

Carey was dismayed to hear the younger twin sound so despondent. “You always get better grades than Zack.” Carey tried to sound reassuring.

“Yeah, like that matters! I want to be good at something that people think is important.”

Obviously, Carey thought that doing well in school was of the utmost importance. But she also knew that wasn’t what Cody needed to hear right now. “And you will be," she said consolingly. "You just have to get out there and find it."

"I don't think it's that easy." Cody shook his head somberly.

"But if you're out there trying, it will find you. You know how singing found me? I entered my high school talent show. You know what my talent was?"

Duh, Cody thought. "Singing," was obviously the answer. His mother was a professional singer, after all.

"No," said Carey. Boy, was her son in for a shock. "Stand-up comedy."

Cody was more than shocked; he was horrified. "But, Mom, you're not funny."

Carey tried to let the insult go. "So, anyway," she continued through gritted teeth, "I'm up there onstage, nobody's laughing, and I panicked. So I just started singing. And you know what?"

"They started laughing?" asked Cody, embarrassed at the thought of his mother making a fool of herself in front of the entire school.

"No . . . I won."

Cody hadn't expected his mom to say *that*! "Wow!" he exclaimed. "I get what you're saying. I should do something I'm no good at, and hope by accident I find something else."

"That's one way of looking at it," mumbled Carey, wondering if she'd taught her son the right lesson.

Well, at least he looked a little more cheerful. . . .

Chapter 4

"London, don't you think you can help me with some of *your* packages?" wheezed Maddie as she entered the lobby. Judging by the enormous haul, the shopping excursion had been a huge success.

"Sorry, manicure. Still wet." London waved her painted fingers in the air as a reminder. "Didn't you just love hanging out at Nelly's Amazing Nails?"

As much as I love getting the flu shot, Maddie thought. "I held your foot while you got a pedicure," she reminded London.

"I know, wasn't it fun?" chirped London obliviously. "Let's do it again tomorrow."

"I'm busy."

"You're too busy to hang out with someone who lent you money? Someone who helped you realize your parents' dream?"

London had her there. "Okay," Maddie sighed guiltily. "So what are we doing tomorrow?"

"Well, I'm busy, but you can pick up my dry cleaning. Toodles." Then, London was gone, leaving Maddie to lug the enormous load of shopping bags and boxes up to London's suite.

Maddie caught the eye of Esteban, the Tipton's ever-present bellhop. He rolled his eyes in her direction. "Maddie, why do you let London treat you like a cute blond pack mule?" he asked.

"I borrowed some money from her and used it to buy the tickets for my parents' trip to Paris," Maddie explained. "Now I'm paying for it in blood, sweat, and tears."

❖❖❖

Esteban didn't have long to contemplate Maddie's sad plight, because he was soon confronted by another odd scene: Cody emerged from the elevator, wearing a suit and carrying a ventriloquist's wooden dummy. What was going on with the kids at this hotel?

"Hi, Esteban," squawked Cody in a voice not his own. Apparently, he was trying to make it seem like the dummy was talking, because the dummy's mouth was moving—though not in time to the words Cody was speaking.

"Oooh, it's a little man! And he's carrying a little man!" Esteban exclaimed. "Oooh, I love your hair."

"Thanks," said Cody.

Esteban shot him a look. "Oh, no, I was talking to the littler man," he said. The dummy had a head full of spiky red hair.

"I think I have found my talent," Cody boasted. "It's ventriloquism. I got this guy cheap because he scares children."

Cody seated himself in a nearby chair and grabbed a cup that just happened to be on the table next to him. He launched into his routine, though he clearly hadn't gotten a handle on ventriloquism yet. Cody's lips moved when the dummy talked, while the dummy's lips moved when Cody talked.

"Hello, Throckmorton," said Cody to the dummy.

"Hello, Cody," said Cody as the dummy.

"Tell me, Throckmorton, you know where cows go on dates?"

"The *mooooo*vies!!!!!!" howled Cody.

Esteban tried to be nice. "That was wonderful!" he said, complimenting Cody on his little performance. "It is amazing how your lips and his move at the same time."

But Cody looked disappointed. "That's not s'posed to happen," he said.

"Oh. Well . . ." said Esteban, searching for something polite to say. Apparently he couldn't think of anything. "In that case, you are no good," he said abruptly. "I am off."

"I guess you're not my talent," a frustrated Cody told the dummy.

"Ya think?" the dummy shot back.

A voice from above sounded stern. "Please, no vaudeville in the lobby." Cody peered up to see Mr. Moseby staring down at him.

Cody didn't have it in him to argue. "Just take him," he said glumly, handing the dummy over to Mr. Moseby. "He's yours."

Chapter 5

Okay, so maybe Cody didn't have the stuff to be a ventriloquist. But he wasn't giving up on finding his talent just yet.

The next day, he entered the bathroom wearing a top hat and a suit, a fanned-out deck of cards in his hand.

"Ahhhh!" screamed a voice from behind the shower curtain. It was Carey.

"Pick a card," Cody told his mother.

"You may have not noticed," said the muffled voice, "but I'm in the shower."

"I think I finally found something I might be good at. But I need your help. So, pick a card, any card." Cody did an elaborate shuffling maneuver with his right hand.

Carey reached her wet, soapy arm out and picked a card.

"Is it the three of diamonds?" Cody asked.

"No," said Carey. "King of clubs."

Cody stamped his foot on the tiled floor. It made a gushy sloshing sound. "It should have been the three of diamonds," he muttered in frustration. "Where'd it go?"

He scrounged around for the right card as magic items of all sorts fell from his jacket pockets: dice, coins, scarves. "Oops," said Cody, looking at the mess he'd made. "That's not s'posed to happen."

❖❖❖

Downstairs, in the hotel ballroom, the TV crew for *Go Dance USA* was preparing for auditions, while contestants practiced their routines. "All right. Test one, two. Test!" the producer shouted into the microphone.

London, seated at the celebrity judges table, mistook the producer for a contestant practicing a routine. "Oh, you're horrible!" she criticized. "You're gonna kill the show. And aren't you a little too old to be a contestant?"

"That's not a contestant, that's the producer," Maddie whispered.

The producer? As in the big cheese? The boss? A mortified London made a desperate attempt to save face. "Kidding!" she called out. "Love the dress!" Then she turned to Maddie, with an accusing look. "Why didn't you stop me?" she said, seething.

"I didn't know you were going to say something stupid," Maddie balked. Then, because she couldn't resist, she added, "Well, yes, I did."

London was offended. "Is that any way to talk to a friend you owe money to?" she gasped.

London had her there . . . again. "You're right, I'm sorry," Maddie apologized. "Can I get you anything?"

"Caramel mochaccino latte," snapped London, who waited until Maddie had walked several feet to add, "Oh, and Madeline, I'd also like a biscotti. Be sure to scrape the chocolate off. Thanks."

As Maddie was stalking off, Esteban intercepted her. Apparently, he'd heard everything. "Maddie," he said, "I can watch this no longer. London is treating you like a dog."

"Huh, I wish," Maddie scoffed. "No, her dog's upstairs in the hot tub. Which reminds me . . . I have to give her a massage."

Esteban could barely take hearing this. "I cannot believe she is making you give her shih tzu a shiatsu," he remarked sadly.

Maddie shrugged. "Yeah, well, until I give her her two hundred fifty dollars back, I'm scraping biscottis."

Like Maddie, Esteban was a hard worker. He didn't like seeing her abused. "Yes, but you are better than that," he insisted. "You must have self-respect. You must have dignity. You must never, never kowtow to anyone!"

It was at this very moment they heard Mr. Moseby, otherwise known as Esteban's boss, scream in his shrillest tone: "Esteban, I need you!"

Esteban needed to show Maddie what it

meant not to take abuse. "When I'm good and ready!" he boldly responded.

"What did you say!?" huffed a furious Mr. Moseby.

Esteban didn't want to seem like a hypocrite. Then again, he needed his job. "Now I'm good and ready!" he yelled to his boss, and sped off, leaving Maddie to her errands.

Chapter 6

Cody was still up in the suite. "Come on, honey," called Carey, "the dance contest is about to start."

But Cody had something to show his mother first. He held a newspaper cone in one hand and a pitcher of milk in the other. "And you are about to be amazed," he announced.

"Oh, no," groaned Carey, glancing at her

watch. She wanted to support Cody, but not at the expense of missing Zack's audition.

"Oh, yes," said Cody, pouring the pitcher into the cone. "The disappearing milk trick." He unfurled the newspaper cone. It was empty! Cody made a "ta-da" type of motion with his hand. "And there's no milk in the cone!" he yelled in triumph.

"That's because it's in my shoes," Carey grumbled, staring at the puddle of milk forming on the floor.

"Yes," said Cody, trying to cover for the trick having gone awry. "It's the old milk-appearing-in-the-shoes trick."

Carey nodded, then went to her bedroom to change her shoes.

A couple of hours later, the contest was over and auditions were complete.

"The votes are in," announced the emcee.

"Our finalists are . . . Dick and Perry, Bud and Lou, Charlie and Lynette, Jan and Dean . . . and . . .

". . . Max and Zack! See you on Saturday!"

"Yes! We made it to the finals!" Max shouted gleefully. "Zack, you rocked!"

Carey offered them congratulations. Cody offered them a cane. "Have a flower," he said, expecting one to pop out of the cane—he'd studied the trick just that morning! Cody gave the cane a tap. Then he gave it another tap. Arrrgh . . . nothing was happening. "Or a cane," he muttered in defeat.

❖❖❖

That evening, the auditions behind them, Zack and Max were buzzing with anticipation. "Oh, and another thing," said Max,

"London said we need a new wardrobe. Something more fabulous. Something more ta-da-ish."

"Great," said Zack, who was less interested in clothes than dessert. "Let's start with some ice cream."

But Max had some bad news for him. "No ice cream for you, pal," she said. "You'll get fat. You're in training."

"Then I'll skateboard over to get the ice cream."

"No, no, no. We have a shot at this title. That means no skateboarding, no Rollerblading, no basketball—you could get hurt." Max was really taking this contest seriously. "Practice!" she ordered.

Then, lightly punching Zack in the stomach, she added, "And lay off the fries!"

Those were her last words before leaving the suite to go home.

"She can't tell me what to do," Zack complained.

Cody was nearby, smirking. Watching Max order Zack around had been the bright spot in a superlame day.

Now Zack was on a rant. Clearly, he did not take well to being bossed around. "If I wanna skateboard, I'll skateboard!" he declared. "If I wanna jump on the bed, I'll jump on the bed."

To prove his point, he got on the bed and started jumping. "Oooh, look," Zack mocked in his whiniest voice. "I'm jumping on the bed. I'm gonna hurt myself. I'm gonna hurt myself."

And then, Zack took a really big bounce.

A supersized bounce.

A mega-fantastic, triple-bombastic bounce that sent him flying into the air and careening over the side of the bed. At first, there was just silence, and then . . .

Crash!

"Oooh, I hurt myself," a small voice moaned.

Chapter 7

"Cody, don't tell Max I hurt my ankle," Zack pleaded. He was clutching his ankle, which was throbbing with pain.

"You're gonna have to tell her sometime," warned Cody.

Zack, who wasn't scared of many things, looked suddenly petrified. "No, she'll beat my insides out, and I like my insides in!"

Cody reached down to help Zack up.

"Well, she kinda might figure it out when she's dancing alone," he said.

"But she won't be dancing alone," said Zack, now on his feet. He could barely walk; in fact, he could barely limp. But apparently, he could still scheme.

Cody wondered if maybe Zack had hurt his head, too. "What are you talking about?" he asked his brother. "There are no substitutions. You'll be disqualified."

Zack got a sneaky glint in his eyes. "Not if the substitute looks exactly like the original."

Cody couldn't believe Zack had said what he'd just said! Did he realize who he was talking to? The klutz of all klutzes! "But . . ." Cody could barely spit the words out. "But I can't dance. I can't do anything."

"That's not true," argued Zack. "You're my brother. You have my DNA. You have my face, my arms, my legs, my shirt. Which, by the way, I want back. You can do anything I can do."

Cody liked the sound of that. . . . "Yeah, yeah. I can," he said, sounding bolstered. "And better!"

"Let's not get carried away," laughed Zack. "Just be good enough to win the contest."

"I'll do it!" cried Cody enthusiastically.

"See, Cody, you've finally found your talent! It's looking like me!"

"Yeah—" echoed Cody without really thinking about what his brother had just said.

❖❖❖

The next day, Cody followed Zack's instructions and went to rehearsal. He did his best

Zack strut as he entered the ballroom, and used his best Zack voice to suavely say: "Hey, Max."

It didn't work. Not even for a second.

"Hey, Cody," greeted Max. "Where's Zack?"

Busted already! Drat! Cody tried his best to front. "I'm Zack," he said with a grin. He needed to ham it up. Zack could really work the charm when he talked to girls. "Hey, sweet thang," Cody called out.

Max wasn't buying it. She cut right to the chase. "He hurt himself, didn't he?"

It was no use. "Yup," answered Cody, defeated.

Max looked heartbroken. "What am I going to do about the contest now?"

Cody tried his best to sound encouraging. "Well, I'm gonna take his place and dance with you."

Max quickly nixed that idea. "Not gonna happen," she said.

"Aw, come on, give me a chance," Cody pleaded. "I'll work really hard. Zack talked me through the dance steps. And check out this really great move I've been working on."

Cody put on his game face and launched into a move that involved hopping around like a kangaroo with a swollen knee. His attempt at grace turned into a colossal gaffe as he tripped, falling to the ground. "I call it trip-hop," he joked.

"I call it last place," said Max.

Chapter 8

Maddie dug her thumbs into London's shoulder blades. She'd been giving London a massage for the past hour, and London was still complaining about her various aches and pains. "Being a judge on TV is so stressful," London whined.

"I know, London. Let me wring—" Maddie caught herself. "I mean . . . rub your neck."

London had requested that the massage be administered in the center of the lobby in full view of the hotel's guests and staff, including Mr. Moseby and Esteban.

"What's going on with them?" Mr. Moseby asked Esteban.

"Well, I do not think I should speak about Maddie's personal business with her employer," answered Esteban.

"Don't tell me," said Mr. Moseby with a shrug. Then, as if out of nowhere, he pulled out Cody's dummy, Throckmorton. "Tell the dummy."

That sounded fair to Esteban. "Can you keep a secret?" he asked the dummy.

It turned out Mr. Moseby had a talent for ventriloquism. "My lips are sealed," the dummy promised.

"Good," said Esteban. And he launched into Maddie's woeful tale. . . .

❖❖❖

The day of the *Go Dance USA* contest found Zack lying in bed, unable to move.

"The dance contest is about to start," Carey reminded him. "Don't you want to watch?"

Zack groaned miserably. "Just looking at dancing makes my foot throb."

Carey looked from her injured son to the remote control and shrugged. "Okay, well, close your eyes, because I want to watch."

She turned the TV on. Just in time, too. Because the emcee announced: "Our next Boston duo wowed everyone with their hip-hop dance number."

Uh-oh, thought Zack. *Think fast!*

He put on his best sad voice, turned to his mom, and moaned: "Could you leave the room and get me a glass of water? My ankle's making me thirsty."

"That's an odd way to phrase it," said Carey, "but okay."

But Zack hadn't been quick enough. Carey was still in his room when she heard the emcee say: "Coming up in our next segment, Max and Zack."

Carey stopped moving. "Who and who?" she asked, turning to glare at her son.

"Wax and Fax," Zack lied. "They're great."

"Funny, it sure looks like you and Max," Carey said as she watched Cody and Max, dressed in black blazers and red shirts, waving to the cameras. "How can you be here and there at the same time?"

Oh, shoot! How was Zack gonna get out of this one? "Cody got really good at his magic act?" he faltered. Carey didn't look like she was buying it. Zack resorted to the

“Max and I signed up for a dance contest,” Zack told his mom.

“The *Go Dance USA* one?” asked Carey. “Good for you.”

**"Zack's better at everything than me,"
Cody groaned. "Basketball, skateboarding, guitar,
and now dancing. . . . What am I good at?"**

**"Maddie, why do you let London treat you like
a cute, blond pack mule?" Esteban asked.**

"I borrowed some money from her and used it to buy the tickets for my parents' trip to Paris," Maddie explained.

After Zack hurt his ankle, he had an idea. Cody could fill in for him! "You're my brother," Zack said "You can do anything I can do."

"He hurt himself, didn't he?" Max asked.
"Yup," answered Cody, feeling defeated.

"Aw, come on, give me a chance," Cody pleaded.
"I'll work really hard."

truth . . . well, sort of. "We did it to help our friend," he said.

"If you really wanted to help your friend you wouldn't have been jumping on the bed," said Carey sharply. "Having your twin brother replace you is cheating."

Hey! thought Zack. *This was just as much Cody's fault. Maybe more!* "Why are you lecturing me? Cody's the one down there doing it."

"Not for long," said Carey. She marched out of the room.

Uh-oh, thought Zack, struggling to get up. "Wait, wait," he called to his mom. "Ow. Wait. Ow. Wait. Ow . . ."

❖❖❖

Max and Cody hovered backstage. They were up next. "Remember," instructed Max, "all you have to do is smile, look pretty, and let me do the dancing."

Cody still wanted to give his dance move a shot. "But, but can I do my move?" he asked. "You said yourself I was getting as good as Zack."

"I lied!"

"But my move is really coming along."

Max glared fiercely at Cody. "You make one move I didn't show you, it'll be the last move you ever make!"

And so, Cody agreed not to do the move. As both he and Zack had learned, Max could be very persuasive—and more than a little scary.

Zack and Carey entered the ballroom just as the emcee screamed, "Now let's give a big *Go Dance USA* welcome to Max and Zack!" They took their seats as Max and Cody bounded onstage.

❖❖❖

At first, Cody did as he was told. He stayed virtually still while Max danced around him. He wiggled his foot. He bobbed his head. He shook out his arm.

Something happened when he shook out his arm!

A flower emerged from his jacket sleeve! Cody hadn't realized he'd been wearing the rigged jacket he'd purchased at the magic store!

The audience loved it. The hoots and hollers invigorated Cody. With a small bow, he handed the flower to Max, who put it in her teeth as she continued dancing. Just then, an entire bouquet of flowers popped out of Cody's other sleeve. Cody gave it to Max, who flung it into the cheering audience. This was going brilliantly!

"What's going on?" asked Max under her breath.

"I forgot to unrig my jacket," Cody explained.

They went on with the routine, when all of a sudden a cane popped out of Cody's jacket. Max expertly guided them into a tap-dance move, using the cane as a prop. Max grabbed ahold of Cody's hand, and when she let go, she pulled a scarf out of Cody's sleeve. Another magical element of the jacket! Only it wasn't just one scarf. The scarf was tied to another to another to another, until Cody was tied up in a chain of scarves. A flabbergasted Max, still dancing, didn't know what to do. She had to get him out! She tugged on the chain, and the scarves began to unwind, taking Cody with them. Suddenly, he was spinning like a top.

The audience, who still thought all of this was on purpose, went wild.

"Keep it up, it's workin'," whispered Max when Cody was finished spinning.

Cody couldn't help but "keep it up." He was dizzy from spinning, exhilarated by the roaring crowd, and something was scratching his knee. Were these trick pants, too? Cody started to shake his leg in wild movements. All of a sudden, a rabbit crawled out of his pant leg and scampered across the stage!

The crowd whistled.

They shrieked.

They stomped their feet.

Cody felt a rush of confidence surge through him. "I feel the music in me!" he told Max. "Step off Mama, Daddy gotta dance."

"No, not the move—" begged Max.

But there was no stopping Cody now. He launched into his maimed-kangaroo move, and within seconds was careening into the trophy case, bringing down all the trophies with it. The sound of clanging metal echoed through the ballroom.

Carey leaped to the stage. “Cody! Are you okay?”

Unfortunately, the emcee heard this. “Cody? I thought his name was Zack?”

“No, that’s Zack,” said Carey pointing into the audience. Zack gave a meek smile and wave.

“We’re toast,” groaned Max.

“You’re not toast,” corrected the emcee. “You’re disqualified.”

Chapter 9

Moments later, they converged backstage.

"Mom, don't be mad," pleaded Cody.

"I'm not mad," stammered Carey, "I'm—"

"Furious!" interrupted Max. "I told you not to do the move. And what did you do? You did the move!" She watched bitterly as the winning dance couple walked offstage with their prize. "That dented trophy should have been ours!" Max stormed.

"Max is right," Carey told Cody. Then she turned to Zack. "And you, young man—"

Max took over. "I don't know where to start! Yes, I do. I told you not to do anything stupid, and what do you do? Something stupid! You're worse than Harry Stupidini here!" She pointed to Cody.

"See?" Cody told his mother "He's even better than me at being worse."

Then, Max turned on him. "You know what your problem is?"

Except now Carey stopped her. "Honey, can I take it from here?" she asked.

Max threw up her hands in disgust, wishing Carey good luck. "Maybe they'll listen to you," she said before stomping off.

"Okay, listen, guys, Max pretty much

covered the whole yelling at you part," said Carey. "But there's something else going on here." She turned to Cody. "You need to stop comparing yourself to your brother. You look the same on the outside, but you're different on the inside. It's like pies. One could be apple, one could be cherry."

"Can I have ice cream on me?" asked Zack, his mind *still* on dessert.

Carey wasn't done with Cody, so she sent Zack off to soak his ankle.

"Honey, do you realize that if you hadn't tried to outshine Zack with that move, you might have won . . . and then gotten disqualified."

"Yeah, I was a good dancer, wasn't I?" said Cody.

"But a better magician," said Carey. "And that's what won them over—the thing you can do that Zack can't."

Apparently, Zack hadn't gotten very far because having overheard he couldn't help putting his two cents in. "Although, if I did get one of those jackets—" he remarked.

"Soak! Upstairs!" ordered Carey. She wondered if her boys would ever learn. . . .

Chapter 10

"Madeline, be a dear and fetch me another soda," ordered London. Being a judge could sure make your throat parched!

"Right away, London," said Maddie, shuffling off.

Maddie was on her way to the soda machine, when Esteban, Mr. Moseby, and his constant companion, Throckmorton, confronted her. "Can't talk," bristled Maddie. "London's thirsty."

But Esteban had something important to say. "On behalf of the entire staff, we have raised this money so you can pay back London and look your mirror in the face."

"That is so sweet," said Maddie, "but I can't take this . . ."

A scream came hurling from afar. "Soda, please!" It was London.

". . . without saying thank you," Maddie said, reconsidering. Gripping the wad of cash, she turned to Mr. Moseby. "Did you have anything to do with this?" she asked.

"Actually, I don't get involved in my employees' personal lives," Mr. Moseby said.

"I saw him throw in a hundred bucks," tattled Throckmorton.

"Bigmouth!" scolded Mr. Moseby.

"Well, then, give him this for me," said Maddie, and she kissed Throckmorton's cold, wooden cheek.

"Madeline, still thirsty!" screeched London impatiently.

Maddie was all too happy to hand over the two hundred fifty smackers to London. "Here you go," she said.

"I have money," London whined. "I want a soda."

"No, this is the money I owe you. And now I'm free. I'm free. I'm free at last!" Maddie skipped gleefully around London.

Maddie was shocked to see that London almost looked hurt. "But we were having so much fun," London quivered.

"*You* were having fun," Maddie told her. "I was watching you have fun!"

This didn't make sense to London. "What could be more fun?" she wondered.

"Root canal you don't need?" suggested Maddie.

"I thought we were friends," said London. "I loaned you money."

"London, money can't buy you friends. You make friends by being nice to people."

"But that seems harder," London said, pouting.

Maddie protested. "No, no, no. It's really easy to say nice things to people. Watch. London . . . you are . . . uhhh . . ."

This was harder than Maddie thought it would be!

"Yes?" asked London, waiting.

"Oooh, wait, got one," said Maddie. She turned to London and said, "Deep down I suspect you're a good person."

"Aww. Thank you," said London. Looking touched and all too pleased with herself, she got up and walked away.

"You're supposed to say something nice back!" Maddie called out.

"I said thank you," London huffed.

"You're welcome," muttered Maddie.

Some things never change. . . .

Don't miss the next story about Zack and Cody

Adapted by Beth Beechwood

Based on the television series, "The Suite Life of Zack & Cody", created by Danny Kallis & Jim Geoghan

Based on the episode written by Marc Flanagan

Life at the Tipton Hotel was almost never dull, but today felt pretty boring to Zack. He had a science project to work on with Cody, but that was pretty much the last thing he wanted to do. As he and Cody waited for the elevator in the lobby, Zack tried not to think about the tedious work that awaited him upstairs. He focused on his yo-yo skills instead. When the elevator doors opened, Cody stepped in, but Zack just kept playing with his yo-yo. Cody stared at his brother. "Hey, come on, man," he whined to Zack. "We have to go work on our science project."

"I *am* doing science," Zack explained as he threw the yo-yo out in front of him for the "around the world" trick. "Look, centrifugal force."

Cody had no choice—he would have to go up and start the project himself. His brother was of no use to him right now, anyway.

Zack continued to play with the yo-yo after the elevator doors closed. He was sure Cody could handle the science project by himself.

Meanwhile, London had entered the hotel in a huff. She and her dog, Ivana, were both wearing party hats. As ridiculous as this might have looked on someone else, London managed to carry it off with some degree of authority. Maybe because she also had on a fur shrug and light green tinted sunglasses. She was the picture of trendiness. She crossed over to the candy counter where Moseby was having tea and chatting with Maddie.

"Moseby!" London shouted. She clearly had an agenda and was in no mood for small talk. "Jeny Freiberger just threw the most incredible party for her dog, and Ivana's upset."

"Of course she is." Maddie couldn't resist. It had to be said. "Look at that stupid hat you put on her." London was a good friend, but Maddie enjoyed making fun of her in spite of that fact.

"Cat person," London replied, barely giving Maddie's comment a thought. She was used to Maddie's snide comments about the way she dressed Ivana. She turned her attention back to Mr. Moseby; she knew he would take care of this for her. He had to do what she said: her father was his boss, and Mr. Moseby *lived* to please his boss. "I want a bigger, better party for Ivana, in the grand ballroom. Here's the guest list," she said, handing him a piece of paper.

"I will take care of it personally," Mr. Moseby said. Just as quickly as she had come, London was gone. Mr. Moseby handed the list to Maddie. "Maddie, take care of it personally," he said.

Maddie sighed. She always got these kinds of jobs. "No one else will touch it?"

"Not with a ten-foot pooper-scooper," Mr. Moseby replied.

Just then, Esteban ran up to them, waving a piece of paper. "Mr. Moseby! You received a fax! The Tipton Hotel inspector is on the way for a surprise inspection."

Moseby wasn't terribly concerned. "How can it be a surprise inspection if they sent a fax?" he asked.

"Because the fax came two weeks ago and I forgot to give it to you. Surprise!" Esteban said meekly. He was always so eager to please his boss, but this time he had screwed up. He felt terrible. Luckily, Mr. Moseby relieved him of his guilt immediately.

"Fortunately for all of us, my hotel is always in tip-top Tipton shape and nothing has changed since the last inspection." But not everything was the same as last time. Just as Mr. Moseby finished his sentence, a certain yo-yo came sailing through the air, landing smack in his teacup. With tea splashed across his face, Mr. Moseby glared at Zack and said, "Except for that."

Without realizing it, Zack had reminded Mr. Moseby of exactly what had changed. He made a run for it.

❖❖❖

Cody was busy working on his science project at the kitchen table when Carey entered the room. Muriel, the hotel maid, was cleaning around them.

"Hey, Muriel," Carey asked with some concern. "When you were cleaning in the bedroom, did you see a five-dollar bill?"

"I thought you were throwing that out," Muriel said earnestly.

Carey, knowing who she was dealing with, said, "It was on my dresser." Muriel could be exasperating sometimes.

"My bad," Muriel said matter-of-factly as she handed Carey the bill. Carey eyed the maid, but before she could consider her exchange with Muriel, Zack burst in huffing and puffing.

"Hide me!" he shouted.

"Whoa, whoa, whoa!" Carey slowed her son down. "What happened?"

"Mr. Moseby's after me! Just because I was playing with my yo-yo in the lobby and it might have landed in his mug."

"And then?" Carey asked.

"I ran after that," Zack admitted. "He scares me."

"Mr. Moseby is just doing his job. He needs to keep this hotel running smoothly, and you tend to be . . ." Carey paused for a moment, trying to think of the right word. "Un-smooth," she finished, smiling.

"Yeah, smooth like Mom when she doesn't shave her legs for two weeks," Cody joked.

Carey wasn't amused. Her mouth was agape at her son's comment. "Aren't you two supposed to be working on your science experiment?"

"We've already started. Look!" he said, opening the cabinet. Inside were two cages, each with a rat inside. Carey was so horrified she jumped up on a chair and started screaming hysterically.

"Aaaaaaaaahhhhhhhhh! No, no, no! What . . . what are you doing with those rats?"

"Science," Zack replied, as if it were so obvious.

"We got these from our school," Cody explained further. "This is Bonnie and that's Clyde. They're our experiment."

"Which is what?" Carey said, still shaky. She stepped off the chair, cautiously. "Giving your mother a heart attack?"

"No, I play rap music for Bonnie and heavy metal for Clyde, and then Cody writes down some scientific stuff."

"You know, behavioral changes . . . like eating habits, mood swings, urination patterns—"

Carey interrupted him. "Ewww! Why does it have to be rats?" She was wiping herself all over, trying to get the grossness of the situation off.

"Too late now," Zack said, "we've bonded." He hugged one of the cages affectionately.

"Swell," said Carey, picking up the cages. "Well, if you don't mind, I'm going to take Bonnie and Clyde away from where we eat." She was carrying the cages with just two fingers, holding them as far away from herself as possible. When she was gone, the doorbell rang.

"I'll get it," Cody said.

"No, wait. What if it's Mr. Moseby? I'm toast."

Cody thought about that for a second. He decided he had no problem with that scenario. "Come in!" Cody shouted happily. Moseby entered their suite with a big smile on his face. Zack immediately felt the need to explain himself.

"Look, Mr. Moseby, about that yo-yo—"

But for once, Moseby didn't seem mad . . . at all. "Oh, pish-posh," he said with a little too much enthusiasm in his voice. "Boys will be boys. You were just having fun, and that's what boys do, isn't it? They have fun!"

Zack stared at Mr. Moseby. Had he gone crazy? "Did that yo-yo bounce off your head?"

"No. I'm fine. I came up here to offer you

scamps tickets to today's Red Sox game. It's a matinee." Mr. Moseby handed the boys the tickets, and they couldn't contain themselves. They actually jumped up and down!

"The Sox game?!" Cody yelled. "All right!"

"Yes, and your seats are just above that little hut wherein the players spit and scratch themselves," Mr. Moseby said. Now Zack was suspicious. This just didn't add up. Only a few minutes ago, he had splashed Mr. Moseby in the face with hot tea. Now, the man was giving them Sox tickets—right above the dugout. Something was up.

"Hold on. There's something wrong here," Zack insisted.

"Why do you question my generosity?" Mr. Moseby asked, clearly trying to cover something up.

"Yeah," Cody said to Zack, waving the

tickets in front of his brother's face in hopes that he wouldn't ruin this for them. "Why *do* you question his generosity?" He glared at Zack.

"I'll tell you what," Zack said to Mr. Moseby, with a plan in mind, "you go. I think I'll just stay here and hang out in the ol' lobby. Where's my model rocket?" There was no way Mr. Moseby would let that happen. He had to give it up now.

"No! All right, fine," he conceded. "The hotel inspector will be arriving soon and it would be marvelous if you weren't around," he admitted.

"I knew it!" Zack exclaimed. He loved it when his instincts didn't let him down. He considered his situation for a moment. He was pretty sure he had some leverage here. "We'll be 'not around' longer if you throw in a little money for dinner," he said. The boys left Mr. Moseby no choice. He knew what he was up against. He reached into his pocket and handed them some cash.

"I like lobster," Cody said.

Mr. Moseby sighed and handed them more cash. The deal was done—his hotel's reputation was safe. He could breathe a big sigh of relief . . . or at least he thought he could.